W9-AZS-682

Rainy Day Readers

How to Become a Perfect Princess in Five Days

Text by
Pierrette Dubé

Illustrations by
Luc Melanson

alphabet
SOUP
an imprint of
WINDMILL BOOKS
New York

Published in 2010 by Windmill Books, LLC
303 Park Avenue South, Suite # 1280, New York, NY 10010-3657

Adaptations to North American Edition © 2010 Windmill Books

Original title: Comment devenir une parfaite princesse en 5 jours
Original Publisher: Les éditions Imagine inc
© Pierrette Dubé / Luc Melanson 2006
© Les éditions Imagine inc. 2006
English text © Les éditions Imagine inc. 2006

Publisher Cataloging in Publication

Dube, Pierrette, 1952-
        How to become a perfect princess in five days. – North American ed. / text by Pierrette Dubé ; illustrations by Luc Melanson.
p.   cm. – (Rainy day readers)
Summary: Young Princess Stringbean, who loves to run everywhere she goes, attends the Perfect Princess Academy with less than perfect results.
ISBN 978-1-60754-376-3 (lib.) – ISBN 978-1-60754-377-0 (pbk.)
ISBN 978-1-60754-378-7 (6-pack)
        1. Princesses—Juvenile fiction   2. Individuality—Juvenile fiction
[1. Princesses—Fiction   2. Individuality—Fiction   3. Conduct of life—Fiction]   I. Melanson, Luc   II. Title   III. Series
        [Fic]—dc22

Printed in the United States of America

For more great fiction and nonfiction, go to windmillbooks.com.

To Marie-Ève, my little princess who runs very

Pierrette

For Mél

Luc Mela

Princess Stringbean was not tiny, not cute, and not graceful. She was tall, clumsy, and tousled. She did not have long blond hair that shimmered like a field of wheat, nor did she have rosey cheeks or sky blue eyes. But Princess Stringbean had the longest legs imaginable and was unbeatable in a foot race.

Every morning, after breakfast, she would put on her princess dress and her princess shoes. That is because princesses never get dressed any other way, she was told. She would put her tiara on top of her wild, wavy red hair because she was told princesses never go anywhere without their diamonds.

Then she announced, "Mommy, I'm going out!"

The moment her feet hit the dirt, she was ready to go! First at a canter, then at a trot, she would circle the castle to warm up. One time, two times, three times.

Next, she worked herself up to a full gallop, crossed the little bridge, climbed up the hill and down the other side.

She raced across the fields and meadows and went through the village, waving at everyone she passed. The villagers were very proud of their princess. When they saw her run past, they would think to themselves that there were lots of pretty, little princesses who sat around looking pretty, but there was no other princess who could run so fast!

However, Princess Stringbean's mother did not share this opinion. When her daughter returned from her morning jog, her hair unkempt and out of breath, Queen Bergamot would be very discouraged at the sight of her. "When will you stop this running? Didn't I tell you a thousand times that princesses take little steps when they walk, and they don't get dirty, and they never wreck their silk dresses? My poor daughter, what will I do with you?"

The queen had great hopes that her daughter would grow up to be like her cousin, Princess Muggins. So pretty and refined.

The queen thought she had found the answer one morning when she received a flyer in the mail, advertising:

Perfect Princess Academy

Become a perfect princess in just

5 Days

or your money back!

"Here is what she needs!" said the queen and she quickly enrolled her daughter.

Princess Stringbean left for school the following Monday. As soon as she felt the dirt under her feet and the rain on her cheeks, she rocketed off, tearing down the road to the next town. Several times she took shortcuts through the woods, jumped a few fences, and leapt over brooks and streams.

Finally she arrived in the schoolyard of the Perfect Princess Academy.

Her entrance caused a bit of a stir.

14

On Monday Madam Grip said, "Today you will learn to put your hair in a neat and tidy little bun and keep your neck straight so that your tiara will not fall off." There was an explosion of pins, combs, and ribbons as each apprentice princess got to work. Princess Stringbean really wanted to put her hair into a pretty round bun, but her hair wouldn't cooperate. Madam Grip was disappointed with the result.

As she fell asleep that evening, Princess Stringbean told herself it would be easier the next day.

On Tuesday Professor Bumblebee said, "Today you will learn to sit without moving and listen to very long speeches. It is very important that you look interested the entire time!" Professor Bumblebee talked and talked, his voice soon becoming a vague buzz. Princess Stringbean really wanted to listen and appear interested, but her eyes didn't. When her chair loudly hit the ground, she was very embarrassed. She told herself things would most certainly go better tomorrow.

Boom!

On Wednesday Mr. Polka said, "Today you will learn to waltz while counting your steps. One-two-three, one-two-three." Princess Stringbean was very enthusiastic when Mr. Polka extended his arm out to her. She really wanted to count one-two-three but her feet wanted to count much higher! Mr. Polka had to take the rest of the day off.

Princess Stringbean told herself she would do better the next day.

On Thursday Madam Buttercup said, "Today you will learn to eat with your mouth shut using a small golden spoon. Each apprentice princess had a pretty, heart-shaped mouth and took only tiny bites. But Princess Stringbean had a big mouth and giant teeth and a big appetite. She really wanted to eat using a little golden spoon but her stomach did not.

That evening Princess Stringbean was worried when she went to bed. "My mother will be disappointed if I do not get my diploma for being a perfect princess," she thought.

On Friday Madam Fru-Fru said, "Today you will learn to descend a long staircase in your evening gown, with the grace and elegance of a perfect little princess." Madam Fru-Fru went first, followed by all the apprentice princesses. "I will get a higher grade if I get down the stairs first," thought Princess Stringbean. But that was not such a good idea.

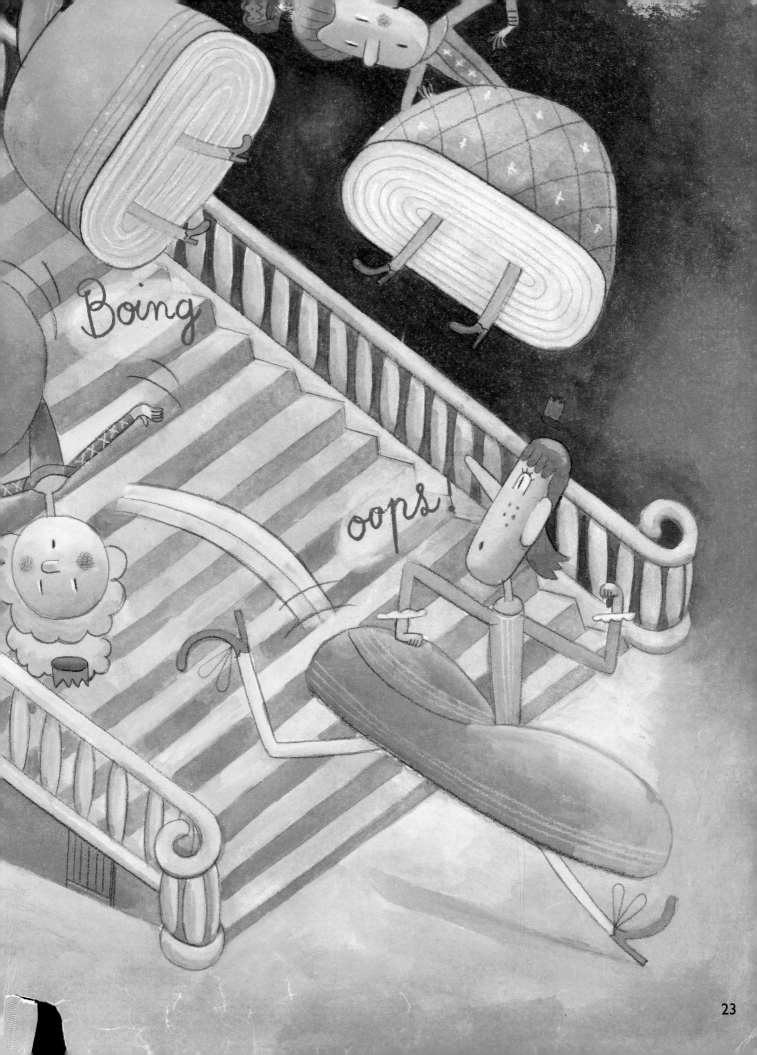

23

That evening, there was a great ceremony, where each and every princess received her diploma in a silver frame. Well, almost every princess did. Princess Stringbean shed a few tears when all she got was a piece of paper that announced she would receive a full refund.

When she left the academy to return home to the castle—cantering, trotting, and galloping—Princess Stringbean was so lost in thought that she took the wrong shortcut. She ended up in a group of knights who also appeared to be in a hurry.

To her great surprise she received a giant trophy! Nothing
like that had ever happened to her!